CARL NORAC   INGRID GODON

My Grandpa
is a
CHAMPION

MACMILLAN CHILDREN'S BOOKS

In memory of Léon:
the kindest grandpa in the world ~ C.N.

First published 2007 by Macmillan Children's Books
a division of Macmillan Publishers Ltd
20 New Wharf Road, London N1 9RR
Basingstoke and Oxford
Associated companies throughout the world
www.panmacmillan.com

ISBN: 978-0-230-01436-7

1 3 5 7 9 8 6 4 2

A CIP catalogue record for this book
is available from the British Library.

Printed in Belgium by Proost

My grandpa doesn't have
lots of trophies or medals.
He doesn't need them.
He's a champion anyway.

He's the champion at blowing up my beach crocodile. He has more puff than anyone else!

And he's the champion at fixing things. He can fix clocks, teddy bears, toys . . . everything.

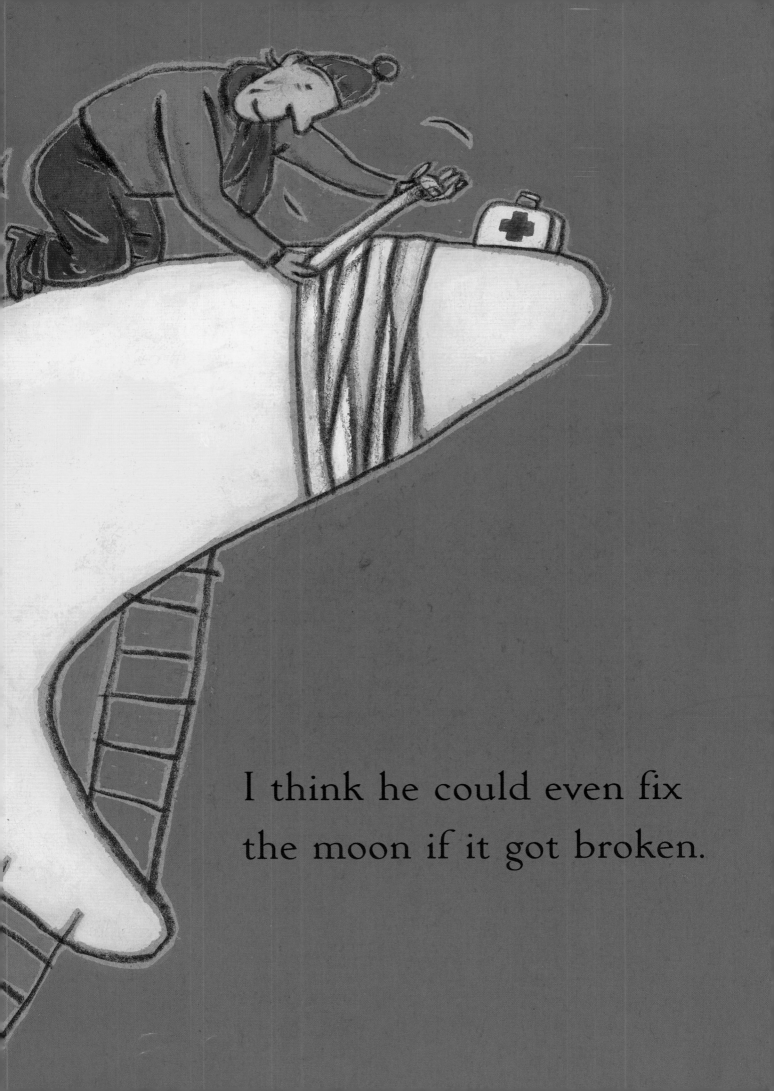

I think he could even fix
the moon if it got broken.

My grandpa is the champion at making me laugh. The funniest thing is when he pretends to ride my toy horse.

And he's a champion at smiling.
When he smiles, everything
he touches smiles too!

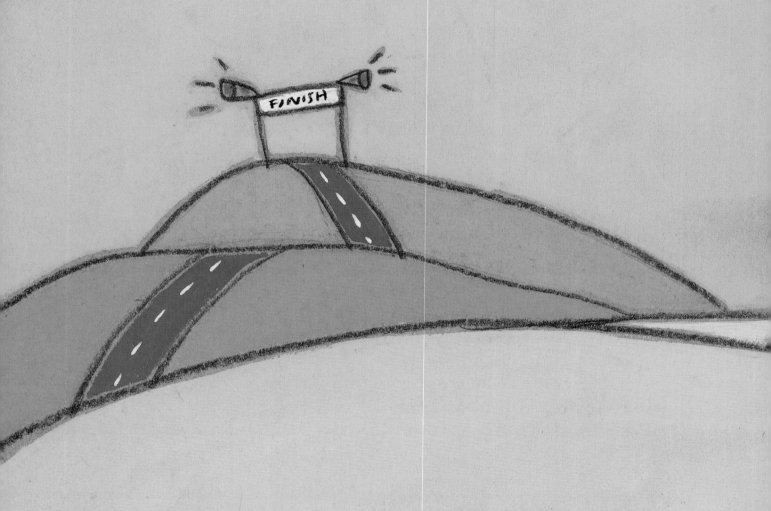

Sometimes my grandpa goes
cycling with me. He cycles
super fast, even up hills!

I think he must be training
for the World Grandpa
Championships.

We often go for walks together.

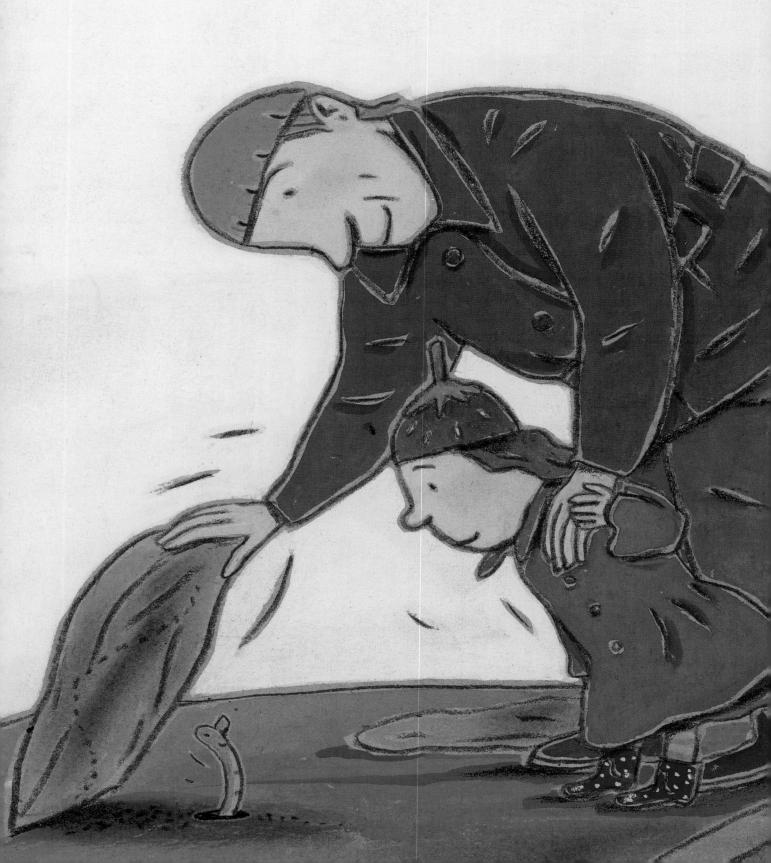

My grandpa is the champion at finding hidden treasure.

He's also the best at spotting
unusual things — like monsters
and dragons in the sky!

But there's one thing that my grandpa can't do as well as me. When he loses his glasses, *I* always find them first!

I like going fishing with my grandpa. If there were a world record for catching strange fish, he would hold it!

But my favourite thing is when my grandpa pushes me on the swings. Then *I* feel like a world record holder.

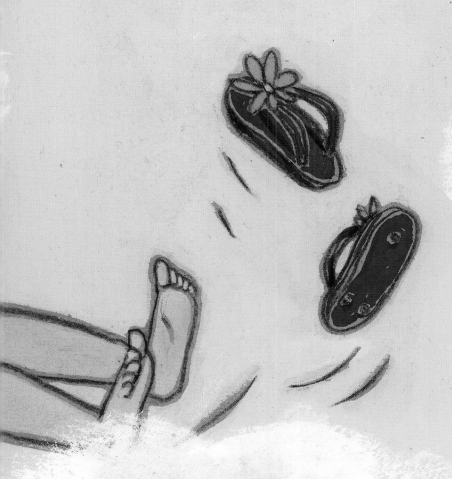

I swing so high I nearly touch the sky!

I'm always happy when my grandpa
whispers special messages to me.

Best of all is when he says,
"I love you, my little champion."
Then I whisper back,
"I love you too, Grandpa!"